LOVE ON THE RUN

A Clean Romantic Suspense

LORANA HOOPES

Copyright © 2020 by Lorana Hoopes

All rights reserved.

No part of this book may be reproduced in any form or by any electronic or mechanical means, including information storage and retrieval systems, without written permission from the author, except for the use of brief quotations in a book review.

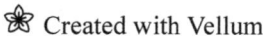 Created with Vellum

PROLOGUE

Ginny Darling paused as she heard the engine of a car outside the window. He couldn't be home. Not yet. She'd thought she had an hour at least. It wasn't much time, but she had decided it would have to be enough. Her eyes darted around the tiny bedroom as she looked to see where she could hide and what looked out of place.

The engine faded away as it continued down the street, and Ginny's breath escaped in a relieved rush. No time to slow down though. This was her one shot. She would not get another one. Quickly folding the shirt in her hands, she shoved it into the suitcase and turned to the dresser to grab some more clothes.

She didn't have many. He only allowed her to have the clothes he purchased for her - none of which were her style, but that had never mattered to him. One day, when she was out from under his thumb and had enough money, she would buy clothes she liked. Simple ones that didn't hug her waist or dip too low.

When her meager outfits were packed, she grabbed her hairbrush and toothbrush out of the bathroom. Nothing else in the bathroom belonged to her. He didn't let her have a curling iron for fear she might use it on him. Nor did he allow her a hair dryer though she was unsure what the fear behind it was unless he thought she might try to throw it in his shower.

She grabbed a towel and a washcloth as well, unsure of how long it would be before she would have the money to purchase her own. Besides, he would be madder that she had gone than that she had taken toiletries.

Ginny hurried to the kitchen to grab food and the little money she had managed to stash away. He didn't let her work, but he did give her money to buy groceries once every two weeks, and every once in a while, she could find a coupon or a deal and end up with a little left. She'd begun stashing it in a container that once held prunes knowing he would never look in it. His aversion to anything healthy would keep him away.

She grabbed it from the shelf along with some crackers and pop tarts. Not the healthiest fare by far, but it would do until she could afford more. Maybe she'd be lucky enough to find work in a restaurant and they would let her take home the extra food. After shoving the food and the can of money into her shoulder bag, she took one final look around the apartment.

It had never been home, not since the first time he had hit her, but it had been a roof over her head and protection from the even rougher crowd on the streets. She hoped she wouldn't end up on the streets again, but she would know better what to look for this time, how to avoid another man like Carl, like her father.

A glance at her watch revealed she needed to get going. If all went well, Carl would be gone another half hour but occasionally his errands ran shorter, and she needed to be gone before he got back.

Adjusting the bag on her shoulder one more time, she grabbed the suitcase and exited the apartment building. Ginny was certain that Carl had neighbors that kept tabs on her comings and goings. The suitcase would definitely arouse suspicion, but she hoped to be at the bus station and on a bus before they could alert Carl.

She kept her ears open and her eyes alert as she made her way to the bus station. Every glance flashed her direction sent her heart racing and her pulse thundering in her ears.

"Where to?" the operator asked when she finally approached the window. His eyes barely registered her, and his tone declared his boredom.

Ginny could not have been more thankful. He would

probably not remember her, and if he did, she doubted he would be able to describe her.

"How far can I get with forty-five dollars?"

His eyes flicked to her for a moment before he leaned forward and tapped on the keys of his computer. "Fire Beach, Illinois, and the bus leaves in ten minutes."

Illinois wasn't as far as she would have liked, but it would have to do. "I'll take one ticket." She placed the few wadded bills she had on the counter and pushed it toward him. A moment later, she held a ticket in her hand. Hopefully, it was her ticket to freedom.

1

GINNY

The bus pulled into Fire Beach, Illinois a little after five. Ginny's stomach rumbled. She'd eaten a pop tart and some crackers on the way, but her stomach was craving real food, especially protein. Unfortunately, she had little money left. She'd have to ask around about a job first and hope she could score some food after.

When the bus stopped, she grabbed her bags and stepped off. The bus station of Fire Beach didn't look much different than the one she had left in Indiana except that she could hear water. She briefly wondered how far the beach was. Perhaps one day, she would be able to enjoy it, but that day was not today.

She scanned the area and noticed a woman sitting on a bench with a notepad on her lap. With no luggage near her, it was a safe bet that the woman lived locally. Ginny bit her lip but decided to approach her. "Excuse me, do you live around here?"

The woman glanced up and offered a friendly smile. "I do. What can I do for you?"

"I just got into town and I'm hoping to find a job. Do you know of any place that's hiring?"

The woman's gaze searched Ginny's face, making her want to squirm under the discerning eyes. With a stylish shirt and smartly tailored pants, this woman looked so put together that Ginny felt even frumpier. She'd put on her most modest shirt and the nicest pair of pants she had, but it didn't hold a candle to this woman's polished look.

"Actually, I might know of just the place. My name is Tia. What's yours?"

Ginny paused as she thought about the question. Should she give her real name? It would probably be required to get a job, but it would also make it easier for Carl to find her. Still, this woman was offering to help her. Honesty seemed like the best option for now, and then perhaps she could ask whoever hired her to call her something later. "It's Ginny. Ginny Darling."

A wide smile split Tia's lips, and her eyes twinkled. "Ginny Darling. That is a great name. It sounds like it came right out of a book."

Ginny wanted to roll her eyes. If her name were in a book, it wouldn't be a nice one. No sweet romance or fantasy book for her. No, since her mother passed away, it had been one punch after the other. She'd survived her father's drunken rages until she was eighteen and legal to be on her own. Unfortunately, she hadn't been the best at managing finances when she first left home, and she'd ended up losing her apartment and walking the streets. And then Carl had found her. She suppressed a shudder and tried to force a smile. "Thank you, I think."

A silvery laugh bubbled out of Tia's throat, and she shook her head as she stood. "I'm sorry. I'm an author and I see stories everywhere. In fact, that's what I was doing here. People watching."

"People watching?" Ginny wasn't sure she had heard the woman correctly.

"Yep. I like to go to public places and watch people. How they walk, their mannerisms, their reactions. Then I try to use those same characteristics when I write my characters. I feel like it makes them more real."

"Ah, that makes sense." Ginny loved books. It was the one thing Carl had allowed her. In addition to her grocery runs, she'd been allowed to visit the local library and check out books. As long as they didn't keep her from keeping the house clean, and she stopped reading when he returned home. She wasn't sure she could even count how many books she had read in the last year. "I do love reading."

"I do too," Tia said with smile. "It's a bit of a walk to

the place I'd like to take you, but it's relatively flat. Are you up for it?"

"Definitely," Ginny said with a swift nod of her head. The sooner she got to this place, the sooner she might get a job and something to eat. Of course then she had to find a place to stay, but she figured she could take one worry at a time.

2
GRAHAM

Graham smiled as he recognized the blonde woman entering Fire Dreams. She had been a hostess with them while getting back on her feet, and though she still stopped in often, it wasn't the same without her sweet smile lighting up the place.

"Tia, good to see you. Table for two?" He didn't recognize the woman with Tia, but that wasn't unusual. Fire Beach had a large population, and in Tia's line of work, she often lunched with editors or publishers from other areas. Although this woman looked too simple to be in the publishing business.

Tia turned to the woman. "Are you hungry? I don't mind grabbing an early dinner if you are."

The woman's face turned a bright shade of red, and her

eyes dropped to the floor. She mumbled something under her breath, and while Graham didn't catch all of it, Tia must have because she smiled and nodded at Graham. "Yes, we'll take a table for two and some of your time if you have it."

Graham glanced around the restaurant. It wasn't quite dinner time yet, so the place wasn't full, and he had a few other people working as well. Besides, his curiosity was piqued now. There was no way he would say no. "I can probably give you a few minutes."

After grabbing two menus from the podium, Graham led the way to a booth near the back. Somehow, he felt the women might need a little privacy. "How about I get us some drinks and then I'm all yours until the place gets busy?"

"That sounds great, Graham, thank you," Tia said. "We'll take water for now." The woman with her said nothing as she slid into one side of the booth.

"Three waters it is." Graham sure hoped the silent woman's story was on Tia's topic list. He was certainly curious as to who she was. He filled the drinks quickly and then returned to the booth. Tia scooted in a little so he could sit down next to her.

"Graham, this is Ginny. She's just arrived in town, and she needs a job. A little birdie told me you were looking for some help."

"I see." Graham looked at the woman across from him. She appeared clean but mousy. Her eyes flicked only briefly to his before dropping again to her lap. "Do you have any restaurant experience, Ginny?"

A slender hand reached up and tucked a strand of her brown hair behind her ears. "Um, a little. I worked at a fast food restaurant when I first graduated high school." Her voice was soft and hesitant.

"And how long ago was that?"

Her eyes met his briefly. "Six years ago."

"Have you worked anywhere since?" Tia asked as if hoping she might get more out of the girl.

The girl shook her head once. "I haven't been allowed to."

"What do you mean you haven't been allowed to?"

Ginny looked up and met Tia's questioning eyes. "For the last few years, I've been living with someone. He didn't let me get a job."

Graham ran a hand across his chin as he and Tia exchanged glances. He wanted to help the girl. It was clear there was something awful in her past, but he wasn't sure he could take a chance on someone who had little experience. Plus, Jordan would give him an earful if he hired the girl without running a background check.

As if realizing what the stretch of silence might mean, Ginny lifted her eyes and held Graham's gaze. "Please. I know you don't me, and I probably sound a little crazy, but I only have a few dollars left to my name. I need a job, so I can afford a place to stay and food to eat. I may be young and inexperienced, but I'm not stupid, and I'll work harder than anyone else."

"And I'll vouch for her," Tia said. "If she doesn't work out or whatever, I'll cover the costs."

Ginny turned her eyes on Tia. "Why would you do that for me? You just met me."

Tia's soft smile held the weight of her story. A story this woman didn't know but Graham did. "Because people did it for me once. They helped me out when I didn't know who I was and when I remembered how awful I had once been." She turned to Graham and fixed him with a pointed stare. "Because that's what we do, right, Graham?"

And just like that he knew he was hiring this girl. Tia was right. They had taken a chance on her - well, Jordan had - and it had been one of their best decisions. If Tia saw something in this woman, then Graham wasn't going to argue with her. She was a pretty good judge of character which is what he would tell Jordan. Hopefully, his brother and co-owner would understand.

"Why don't you two decide what you're eating while I get some paperwork for you to fill out?"

Ginny's eyes widened and glistened with unshed tears. "Really? You're willing to take a chance on me?"

"It's what we do," Graham said as he edged out of the booth. "Just don't make me regret it."

She shook her head. "I won't. I promise."

Graham wasn't sure what that was worth, but he did feel there was something about this woman. Something worth taking a chance on.

3
GINNY

Ginny couldn't believe her luck. Not only had she gotten a job, but Tia had taken her to the local bed and breakfast and introduced her to Cara who owned the place and had offered her a room until she could get out on her own. Ginny couldn't remember the last time she had met such nice people, and she just worried when her bad luck, as it inevitably did, would return.

The walk to Fire Dreams was a few miles from Cara's bed and breakfast, and a light sheen of sweat beaded her forehead as she pulled open the door. Hopefully Graham would understand. She looked around for him as she entered the restaurant, but he was nowhere in sight. However, he had to be somewhere because while the restaurant was definitely not busy, there were a few patrons scattered throughout the place.

Suddenly the sound of raised voices came from the kitchen. She shifted her feet, unsure of what to do. Should she wait? Announce her arrival? The sound of her name took the second option off the table.

"I can't believe you hired her without talking to me. Do you know anything about her?" Ginny didn't recognize this male voice, but she assumed it was Graham's brother who co-owned the restaurant.

"I know that Tia believes her, and I do too. Just meet her, Jordan. You'll see that I'm not wrong about this." That had to be Graham.

"We'll see."

The door to the kitchen flew open and Ginny froze as if her feet were stuck in cement. The man who exited first had brown hair and dark stubble, but it was his fiery eyes that struck Ginny.

"Are you her?" he asked, stopping in front of Ginny.

Behind him, Graham sighed. "Ginny, this is my brother, Detective Jordan Graves. Forgive his rudeness. Evidently, police work is stressful."

Jordan turned his fierce stare on Graham. "You not consulting your partner is stressful." When he turned back to Ginny, his eyes had softened a little, but his presence still commanded attention. "It's nice to meet you, Ginny. I would have preferred to run a background check, but since

Graham and Tia seem taken by you, I'll trust their judgment."

"Um, thank you? I promise you that there's nothing in my past except an abusive ex-boyfriend that I'm trying to get away from."

Jordan's eyebrow lifted. "Do we need to worry about him?"

Ginny shook her head. "I honestly don't know. It depends on how angry he is that I left."

"Okay, well, I'd like his information so I can do some digging and maybe keep tabs on his movement, so if he does come this way, we can be prepared."

"Of course, I'll tell you anything you want to know. His name is Carl Parker, and we lived in Decatur, Indiana."

Jordan issued a nod, promising to return later if he had any further questions, and Ginny sighed as she was left alone with Graham.

"Is he always that intense?"

Graham chuckled. "He's a good guy. He just comes across a little scary sometimes. It helps with his job. He's in the special investigations' unit, but enough about him. Let's get you up to speed on working here."

Ginny kept her focus on Graham as he walked her through the different parts of working in the restaurant. He was going to start her as a hostess, but he also taught her how to clear tables.

"It hasn't been that busy lately, but some nights it will

be. It's important that you don't wait for the busboy if you see that he's busy. Help him out so we can get more people in."

"Yes, sir."

Graham chuckled and pushed the center of his glasses. "You don't need to call me sir. I'm only a handful of years older than you."

"Sorry, I'm just trying to be respectful," Ginny said, softly.

"Hey," Graham touched her arm. "You're doing great. Why don't we call it a day, and I'll see you tomorrow?"

Ginny nodded and tucked a strand of hair behind her ears. "Absolutely, I'll be ready."

4
GRAHAM

Graham watched as Ginny led customers to the table and handed them menus. She seemed to be a natural, picking up everything he had taught her yesterday. He wondered what the rest of her story was as she seemed confident in this role. How had she let a man run her life for so long?

His cell phone buzzed in his pocket, and he pulled it out, wondering what Jordan wanted. He was supposed to work a shift later; he better not be calling to cancel. "Hey, Jordan, what's up?"

"Is Ginny there with you?" Jordan's voice was low and stern.

"Yeah, she's on shift until closing. What's going on?" Graham was used to the many voices of Jordan - his brother had so many different sides, he was more like an octagon than a square - but this was the voice that scared him the most. It was his serious, something bad is about to happen voice.

"I looked into her ex. He's bad news, Graham, and I got word that he left town. I don't know how long it will take him to find her, but my guess is not long. Evidently this guy is pretty well connected in their town, and has a lot of people working for him."

Graham's grip tightened on the phone as he glanced Ginny's direction again. "What do I do?"

"Can you take her to mom's old cabin?"

Graham thought back to the cabin on the lake where they had once gone to get away from the city every year before his father left. He wasn't sure he'd even been out there since their mother passed. "Jordan, it's been empty for ages. There's no food there."

"Actually, there is. I keep it stocked just in case. You'll find everything you need there including a gun in the safe. The combination is Mom's birthday."

Graham shouldn't be surprised by this tidbit of information. The cop in Jordan made him thorough if not a little paranoid. It would be just like him to have a safe house all set up just in case.

"Try to sneak her out the back in case they're already here surveying the place," Jordan continued. "I'll see if Tia can help with the restaurant until you get back, but Graham, you may have to stay there until we catch this guy."

"What about my other job, Jordan? I can't just not show up for work." Graham worked part-time in insurance. He'd cut back his hours at the firm after Fire Dreams began taking off, but he still worked mornings there.

"I'll stop in and let your boss know what's going on. I'm sorry, Graham. If I thought there was another way…"

"It's fine. I'll let the shift manager know and we'll head that way. Just promise me you'll get this guy, Jordan."

"I will."

Graham pocketed the phone and scanned the restaurant as he made his way to Daniel, the shift manager for the night. He was looking for anyone who seemed out of place or nefarious, but the truth was the people after Ginny could be anyone, look like anyone.

When he reached Daniel, he leaned in to keep his voice low and informed Daniel of the situation. "Don't react when we're gone. Just business as usual, got it?"

Daniel nodded, and though his eyes were larger than normal, Graham knew he would do his part. Daniel was ex-military and had a level head.

Graham moved next toward Ginny at the hostess podium. She appeared to be arranging menus and tidying the area, but she smiled as he approached. "Hey, boss, what can I do for you?"

Graham smiled so as not to alarm her. "Hey Ginny. Can you help me with something in the kitchen really quick?"

Her smile faltered the tiniest bit, and he knew she was probably worried she was in trouble. Thankfully, she kept her cool and followed him without protest.

When they were safely in the kitchen, he turned to her. "Jordan just called. Carl's on his way here. We have to go. I can take you somewhere safe, but I need you to come with me. Please?" He held out his hand, knowing he could have demanded but with her past, he had opted to ask, hoping it would show how different he was from her ex.

She looked from his hand to his eyes before nodding. "I trust you, Graham. What do you need me to do?"

"Follow me." He took her first to the break room, grabbing a coat and hat and having her put them on before heading out the back. Perhaps if any of Carl's men were watching the back entrance, it might throw them off. At least long enough for Graham to be out of town before they realized.

He kept his eyes peeled as he led the way to his car. The evening wasn't fully dark yet, and he saw no one looking their direction. Still, he asked Ginny to bend down in the seat so as not to be seen as they drove out of town.

Though he'd never been in a police chase or a tailing,

Jordan had talked about them enough that Graham knew to watch in his mirror for any car that followed them more than two blocks. Thankfully, by the time they drove past the Fire Beach city limit sign, he had seen no suspicious cars, and his heart rate slowed. But only a little.

5
GINNY

"Where are we?" Ginny asked when the car pulled up to a quaint cabin surrounded by trees.

"This is my family's cabin," Graham said as he turned the engine off. "We used to come every summer before…" His voice trailed off as if he didn't want to finish that story. Then he sighed. "I haven't been here in ages."

"Should we have stopped for supplies then?" Ginny asked. She was used to living frugally, but if he hadn't been here in ages, would they even have food?

Graham chuckled and offered a half smile. "You don't know my brother. Evidently, he's been keeping the place stocked. Just in case." He peered into the flower pots lining the porch rail and smiled triumphantly before reaching in one and pulling out a key.

With a slight click, the door opened, and Ginny followed him inside. She'd expected the cabin to smell musty, but while the air was a little stale, it had obviously been aired out recently. "Your brother must come out here often."

"I had no idea he was still coming out here at all until tonight, but it doesn't surprise me. Jordan's always been the one to prepare, to look ahead, and once he became a cop, it was like all signs pointed to danger."

"It must be nice to have someone who looks out for you though," Ginny said as she walked around the living room.

The area was simple with a couch that looked like it could double as a bed and a plush chair. A small table with a lamp on it sat between the two, and there were a few magazines stacked on it. In one small corner was a bookshelf filled with novels, and on the top of the bookshelf was a framed photograph of a man, a woman, and two young boys.

"Is this you?" she asked, holding the picture out to Graham.

His face hardened, and his jaw clenched as he took the picture and set it back on the bookshelf. "Yeah, but that was a long time ago."

"I'm sorry. I didn't mean to pry," Ginny said.

"It's okay." Graham moved away from her and toward the couch. "What about you? Are you an only child?"

"I am. My mother always wanted more children, but she grew sick when I was five, and there was no time. Even when she went into remission a few years later, they didn't try. I think my mother knew her time was limited. She died when I was thirteen." Ginny placed her hands on the back of the chair, unsure if she should sit.

"I'm sorry. My mother's dead too though she lived until I was twenty. What about your father?"

Ginny sighed and bit the inside of her lip. "My father was a great dad until my mother got sick. Then he threw himself into her care. He was a ghost in my life most of those years, but that would have been preferable to what he became after. I think he blamed me for my mother's death. He turned to drinking, and…" Ginny shrugged. "I'm not sure who he was after that."

Graham chuffed and shook his head. "You and I seem to have a lot in common. My father was an alcoholic too. My mother left him when I was ten, and though I visited him after, he never really felt like a dad after that. He died last year and left Jordan and I the restaurant."

A silence descended between them as Ginny was unsure what to say. How had he turned out so much better when their lives were so similar? Was it because he was a boy? Or perhaps because he'd had an older brother who cared for him?

"Speaking of which, I'm getting hungry," Graham said, breaking the silence. "Shall we see what's in the kitchen?"

Ginny followed, and as her stomach rumbled, she realized she hadn't eaten since lunch. She had planned to grab some food during her break as Graham had told her that was allowed, but she'd never gotten the chance.

A surveying of the cabinets revealed that Jordan had indeed stocked the cabin well, and after deciding on chili, she opened the can while Graham found a pot and readied the stove. Though there were no fresh vegetables, she also managed to find green beans and a can of mixed fruit, making her feel as if it was almost a balanced dinner.

When the food was ready, Graham dished the chili into bowls and Ginny placed the green beans and fruit on plates for each of them. They found bottled water in the fridge, and each settled into a chair at the small wooden table.

Ginny reached for her fork, but Graham stilled her hand before she could lift it. "Can I pray for us first?"

"I'm not really the praying type," Ginny said, "but if it makes you feel better then go ahead."

Graham nodded and bowed his head. "Lord, thank you for this food. Thank you for bringing Ginny into our lives. Thank you for this cabin where we could hide out. Please protect us and help us see the blessings amid all the pain. Amen."

Ginny cocked her head as she studied him after the

prayer. "How can you pray after everything you've been through? Your father and losing your mother?"

Graham nodded as if he understood her concern. "I understand where you're coming from. I did stop praying for a time after we left my father, but my mother helped me see that even in the pain, God had plans. She showed me that I could do nothing alone but anything with His help, and she helped me look for the positive. Because of that my brother and I have grown closer, I've met some amazing people, and I've been given the resources to help you and others like you." A soft smile stole across his lips as he shook his head. "If I'd let anger and hatred run my life, I wouldn't have any of those."

Ginny let his words roll around in her head. She thought she had tried to stay positive after her mother died and her father turned in to someone she didn't recognize, but she had certainly never leaned on God. Would her life be somewhere different if she had? Could she still change the trajectory if she followed his approach and stopped trying to do everything on her own? It was definitely something to consider, and she knew she would be chewing over that question long into the night.

6

GRAHAM

Graham gave Ginny a tour of the rest of the cabin after dinner. Not that there was much to it. Two small bedrooms, a laundry room, and a bathroom rounded out the floorplan.

"You can pick whichever room you'd like," Graham said as he opened the door to one of the bedrooms. "This is the one Jordan and I stayed in."

Graham wasn't too surprised to find the room looked exactly the same. A single queen-sized bed sat squarely in the room with a night stand on each side, and a small four-drawer dresser was the only other furniture in the room. "It's not much, but it will do."

"It's more than I've had to myself in a long time," Ginny said softly.

Graham cleared his throat, unsure what to say in

response to that. "Or, option number two is the room my parents shared." He pushed that door open to reveal an almost identical bedroom. The only difference was the bedspread on this bed was covered with flowers instead of a solid blue color like the last room. "I'm afraid we have to share the bathroom, but I'll let you have first dibs."

Ginny's hand flew to her mouth. "I didn't even get to grab my toothbrush or toothpaste."

"Don't worry," Graham said with a smile as he turned on the bathroom light. "If I know my brother, there are probably unopened toothbrushes in here." He squatted down to open the cabinet under the sink and pulled out two brand new toothbrushes and a tube of paste. "Yep, I am never going to get on his case for being so prepared again. Would you like red or blue madam?"

"Mademoiselle," Ginny said with a chuckle.

Graham's face folded in confusion. "Huh?"

"I'm a mademoiselle. Madam's are married, and I'll take red." She plucked the red toothbrush from his hand and held it to her chest like a treasure.

Graham grinned at her comical expression and felt his heart do a funny little dance in his chest. Though she was not classically beautiful, there was something in the innocence and sincerity of her face that he found refreshing and attractive. "Ah, well, you'll have to pardon my rusty French. I took it in high school to woo the ladies, but I haven't had much chance to practice it since."

Ginny's eyes held his gaze as the corners of her lips lifted in a small smile. "Somehow I doubt you had trouble with the ladies in high school or any other time."

"Hah, I was the geeky one. Glasses, see?" He pointed to his face for emphasis. "Jordan was the athletic one who had women swooning all over him."

"Well, as much as I'm sure Jordan is amazing, he's not the one here protecting me right now," Ginny said, pointing her toothbrush at him.

Once again, words failed Graham, and he felt his face heat up. "I'm not sure I'd say protecting. I haven't had to do anything very dangerous yet."

"Let's hope you don't. I'm okay with low-key protecting," Ginny said. "I think I'll take the flowered room if it's okay with you, but I'm not tired quite yet. Is there anything else we could do?"

The way she looked at him was different than any woman ever had. Graham felt as if she could see every part of him, and he wasn't sure what to do with that knowledge. "We could talk? I don't know if there's much else to do. My parents never wanted a TV here, so we wouldn't be tempted to spend our time watching it instead of playing, but we might have some card games still."

Ginny's eyes lit up. "Games? I would love to play a game. My mom and I used to play all the time, but I haven't played any in years."

"A game it is then. Let's see what we have." He led the

way back to his parents' old room and to the small closet that resided there. That was where the games used to be at least. Sure enough, on a shelf was Yahtzee, Skip Bo, Scrabble, and a few others. "What's your poison?" he asked, indicating the games.

Her teeth chewed on her bottom lip as she scanned the offerings. "Yahtzee, please, but we may have to play all of them if we're here too long."

He could not stop the smile that pulled at his lips. "We can play as many as you want."

They set up at the kitchen table and Graham handed her a pad of paper and a pencil. He scanned the paper quickly trying to remind himself of how it was played. It had been ages since he had played any games. In fact, it had probably been since the last summer they were here. His mother had been too busy after that, and Jordan had never really been into games.

"This was the first game my mother taught me," Ginny said softly as she picked up the dice. "She said it would be the easiest because it was just numbers."

Graham chuckled. He liked math, but he had known a lot of kids in school who would have said just numbers was hard enough. "What was your mother like?"

Ginny bit her lip and her eyes glazed over as if focusing on a memory from the past. "She was amazing, although I always remember her being tired. When she first got sick, I couldn't read yet, but she would still let me sit on her lap as she read the unicorn books I loved over and over to me." A slight smile tugged the corners of her lips up. "I used to tell her that I loved her a million percent."

Graham smiled at her, wishing he had the perfect words to say. "I bet she loved that."

Ginny shrugged. "I think she did. Anyway, shall we start?"

And just like that, the subject was closed for now. Graham hoped it would come up again. He sensed there was something special in Ginny but it was hidden behind all her pain. As much as he worried about being away from work and the restaurant, he kind of hoped they would be locked down long enough for her walls to lower.

7

GINNY

Ginny couldn't help staring at Graham as he tapped the pencil's eraser against his lips while deciding where to record his round. He was so unlike Carl or any guy she had dated before, but maybe that was what she found intriguing. Though he did err on the "nerdier" side with his glasses and button-down shirts, he appeared completely comfortable in his skin - something she hadn't been in a long time.

Plus, there was his whole relationship with God. She didn't understand it, but he definitely had a peace that she didn't, even though their stories were similar. He was so different from what she'd known for the last several years that she wanted to know all about him.

"I think I'll take this as three of a kind," he finally said, writing the numbers down.

"Did you and Jordan always get along?" she asked as he pushed the dice in her direction.

A chuff and a slight shake of his head answered her question before his words did. "Not at all. He's older, so he was subjected to my father's drunken rages more than I was and he remembered them more clearly. That kept us apart for a while because he wanted nothing to do with our father, and I just wanted to know him. Plus, Jordan and I are about as different as can be. I'm punctual, and he's always late. I don't mind staying at home, and he thrives on danger. Oddly though, it was the last act of Dad's that drove us together. The restaurant."

"How long have you guys owned it?" Ginny asked as she shook the dice and let them fly across the table. Her eyes widened as she saw four sixes land on the first roll.

"Your luck is looking good tonight," Graham said with a smile. "We've had the restaurant up and running about a year, I guess. We take turns managing it, and we've had to bring in a third shift manager for when Jordan and I can't be there."

"That's amazing. It must be so nice to feel accomplished with something like that." She rolled the lone die once and then again, sighing when it ended up a one. "Guess my luck isn't that good yet."

"Can I ask you something?"

The tone in Graham's voice told her it would be a

serious question and one she probably didn't want to answer, but she found she wouldn't mind telling him the answer to anything he asked. "Sure, go ahead."

"You seem so strong. How did you end up letting a man run your life for so long?" He rolled his dice and marked a full house, not bothering to try and roll again.

Ginny had known this question would come sooner or later. It was the same one she asked herself as well. "I wish I had a good answer for you, but I really don't. When my mom died, my father turned to drinking and he became verbally abusive. I lived with that for five years until I was old enough to move out. I didn't think it had affected me, but that stuff sticks with you." She shook her head and let the dice fly. Twos. Great.

"I took a job waitressing because I thought I'd be amazing, but I had no work ethic. After getting fired, I lost my house and ended up on the streets. That's when you know you've hit rock bottom." She picked up the two dice that weren't twos and threw them again. One more dice landed with a two face up. One more roll. She picked up the last die but paused before throwing it.

"Carl found me on the streets. He was so nice when I first met him. He took me in and provided for me. It had been so long since anyone had done that that I suppose I let myself get lured in. But then he began to change slowly. He stopped taking me places and no longer brought home gifts. If I tried to leave, he would tell me how dangerous it was on the streets and how horrible I was being by rejecting his kindness. It wasn't like I had family or friends out there for me, so it just got easier to stay inside."

Graham sighed and ran a hand across his jaw. "I'm sorry. This lockdown must be hard for you then."

Ginny offered a small smile and shook her head. "It's different. You're so much nicer than Carl ever was, and I know this really is for my safety." She tossed the last die and watched as it teetered on an edge before landing with a two face up. "Yahtzee! Maybe my luck is changing after all."

"I know mine is."

Graham's voice was so soft that Ginny wasn't sure she hadn't imagined it, but when she glanced up, his eyes were locked on hers, and she could feel the intensity.

"Graham, I'm so broken…" Ginny let the words hang in the air, unsure of how to finish them.

"We're all broken, Ginny, but you don't have to stay that way." His hand covered hers. "God can heal those wounds."

Ginny looked down at his hand on top of hers. How long had it been since a man had touched her in that way? With kindness, gentleness, and empathy. "I don't know if I believe in God."

"I can help you with that."

She bit her lip as she considered his words. Was God what made him different? What made him able to see the positive through so much pain? "Maybe I'll let you, but right now, it's your final roll. Let's see if you can beat me."

8
GRAHAM

Graham's eyes popped open, but he wasn't sure why. The light was still mostly dark outside his window, but he could see the first breaks of dawn peeking through. Was it just from sleeping in an unfamiliar bed or was there something more? He held his breath and listened, but the cabin was silent. Still, the feeling did not abate that something was out of place.

Kicking back the covers, Graham swung his legs out of bed and crouched down to retrieve the gun from under the bed. He had placed it there last night after they finished their Yahtzee game. The cabin had been quiet with no signs of Carl or any of his goons, but Graham wasn't going to take any chances.

With the gun at his side, Graham opened his door and

stepped into the hall. The door to the other bedroom was open, and his heart skipped a beat in his chest. Had Carl gotten in without Graham hearing? He was normally a heavy sleeper, but he hadn't felt that he had slept as well last night.

He glanced in Ginny's room, but the bed was empty. Sweat broke out on his forehead as he crept toward the kitchen. Maybe Ginny had just woken early and was having breakfast, but the kitchen was also empty. With no idea where she was, he decided to risk calling out for her. "Ginny?" Silence.

Had she gone outside? Surely, she wouldn't have gone outside alone. The dread deepened in his stomach as he headed for the back door. After slipping on his shoes, he opened the door with as little sound as possible. He had no idea if Carl had taken her or if he might still be here.

The car was still out front and appeared to be in working order. That softened the dread slightly. He rounded the cabin, keeping his eyes peeled for anything out of place and his ears for any sound. As he reached the back of the cabin, he paused. A lone figure stood in the break of the tree line where a slight path led to the small lake situated behind the cabin.

"Ginny?" He said her name softly to avoid scaring her.

She turned and smiled at him. One arm held the other as if she were cold. "I'm sorry. I didn't mean to scare you."

"What are you doing out here, Ginny? It's not safe."

"I know," she shook her head and her hand traveled up to her shoulder, "but it's been so long since I've seen a sunrise. When I woke and realized the sun wasn't up yet, I had to try and see it."

Graham's heart broke at the expression on Ginny's face. What torture must Carl have put her through if she hadn't even been allowed to see the sunrise? He placed the arm not holding the gun around her shoulders and pulled her to him. "It's beautiful, isn't it?"

Honestly, he couldn't remember the last time he had watched a sunrise, but looking at it through Ginny's eyes, he could see the beauty in the reds, oranges, and yellows as they streaked across the sky.

"It sure is."

They stood that way for five or ten minutes just watching the sun rise into the sky and reflect across the placid lake. Though relatively concealed where they stood, Graham still felt exposed, and he finally suggested they go back into the cabin.

With a soft sigh, Ginny allowed him to lead her back. As they reached the side of the cabin where the car was, something caught Graham's eye, and he averted his gaze for just a moment. It was a moment too long as he heard a branch break and felt the cool metal of a barrel against his back before he could turn around.

"Drop it." The voice was low, gravelly, and demanding.

Ginny turned at the sound, and Graham knew when her eyes grew wide and the color drained from her face that Carl had found them. "I'm sorry," he mouthed to her as he dropped the gun to the ground.

"Don't hurt him, Carl." Ginny's voice was small and filled with fear.

"First of all, you don't get to tell me what to do." Though Graham couldn't see Carl's face, he could almost hear the snarl in his voice. "Second, I don't plan to hurt him. I only came to get what was mine."

"She isn't property," Graham said softly.

The gun poked deeper into his back. "You don't get to tell me what she is. I rescued her, so I get to claim her."

"You might have rescued her from the streets, but then you enslaved her in your house." Why was his mouth still going? He was not normally the one who spouted bravery in the face of a gun. That was Jordan's job. He was the one who watched crime shows on his TV and shook his head when the characters did something stupid. Like he was doing now.

"I'm about done with your talking. Ginny, get over here."

"No."

The word was so soft that Graham wouldn't have

believed she had uttered it if he hadn't seen her mouth move.

"What did you say to me?" The gun slid along Graham's back, and he wondered if he could disarm Carl. Jordan had made him learn some self-defense tactics, but did he remember any of them?

"I said no." This time Ginny's voice was more forceful, though Graham could see her shaking. She crossed her arms to try and still the tremors. "You've bossed me around long enough. I don't need you telling me what to do anymore, and I don't want it."

"I paid for you, girl, with every meal and every piece of clothing I purchased for you."

"Clothes I don't even like. You always made me feel like I belonged on the street instead of that you cared about me." She shook her head. "I'm not going back. Not now that I've gotten a taste of freedom."

"Why you little…"

Carl finished the sentence with a guttural growl, but as he did, the gun lifted from Graham's back. He didn't know how, but he just knew the man was raising it to point it at Ginny instead. Adrenaline took over, and he kicked Carl's knee as hard as he could. The man yowled in pain, and a shot exploded from the gun.

A long, continuous ringing took over Graham's hearing, but he didn't let that slow him down. He grabbed Carl's wrist and twisted the way Jordan had shown him until Carl not only dropped the gun but dropped to his knees. Graham pulled both arms behind his back and secured them with his knees.

"Ginny, grab something to bind him with," he hollered behind him.

When he heard no response, he glanced around to see Ginny holding his gun and pointing it at Carl.

"Ginny, no, you're not like him. Let Jordan take care of him." Though the ringing was fading, his words still sounded muffled in his head.

Ginny shook her head, and when she spoke, her words sounded far away. "If I let him go, he'll just keep coming after me. I'll never be free."

Graham shook his head and tried to clear the residual ringing. He needed a clear head to help Ginny understand. "I know you're scared, Ginny, but if you do this, your life will be over too. You'll be no better than him. Please, let Jordan handle this."

The blessed sounds of wheels crunching on gravel carried to Graham's ears, and relief flooded him when Jordan and his partner, Al, stepped out of their car.

As Al hurried his direction to secure Carl, Jordan approached Ginny. "He's right, Ginny. We'll make sure he goes away for a very long time."

"You promise?"

"I do." Jordan placed his hand over Ginny's and took the gun from her.

Al snapped handcuffs on Carl's wrists and hauled him to his feet. "You have the right to remain silent."

She continued, but Graham was no longer listening. As soon as Jordan stepped back from Ginny, Graham wrapped her in his arms. "You okay?"

Her body shook in his arms, but she nodded. "Yeah, I think I'm okay. Thank you. Thank you both."

9

GINNY

Ginny smiled as Graham passed her on his way to the kitchen. It had been a few weeks since the incident with Carl, and Graham had been by her side every day. He'd checked in with her at Cara's Bed and Breakfast and even gone apartment hunting with her when she finally had enough saved to pay the first and last month's rent. He was so different from Carl, from any man she had dated for that matter, and her heart warmed every time she looked at him.

She was fairly certain she was falling in love with him, but she hadn't said the words yet. They had once held such meaning for her before her mother died. Then they had disappeared from her vocabulary until Carl, but he had distorted their meaning. She wanted to be sure that when she told Graham she loved him that it was the pure love and not the tainted kind.

"You seem to be settling in well," Cara said as Ginny led her to a table. There was a handsome man with her, but Ginny didn't recognize him. Of course, only having been in the town a month, there were a lot of people she didn't recognize.

"I am. Graham and Jordan have been amazing bosses, and I can't thank you enough for helping me out when I first got here." Ginny noticed the man with Cara raise his eyebrow at her as he sat down, but Cara just smiled and shook her head.

"It's what I do, and I am always happy to help." Though she had started the sentence while looking at Ginny, she finished it with a pointed stare at her companion. There was obviously something going on between the two, but Ginny didn't know what nor did she want to be in the middle of it.

"Well, thank you. Here are your menus and your server should be with you shortly."

After placing the menus down, she turned and headed back to the hostess podium. Graham stood there smiling at her. "Hey, can you meet me in the kitchen when you get off?"

"Sure, but I still have ten minutes," Ginny said. Though she and Graham were dating, she didn't want special treatment. This was her first job in years, and she wanted to feel like she earned it.

"It's okay. What I have to show you won't expire." With a lopsided smile, he squeezed her hand and then walked away.

Ginny sighed. She was normally a patient person, but now she was curious and the clock never moved faster when she wanted it to.

When her time was up, she forced her feet to walk slowly to the kitchen though every part of her wanted to skip or run. She pushed open the door and paused when she saw both Graham and Jordan waiting for her. Was she in trouble? She couldn't think of anything she had done wrong and Graham had seemed pleased when he spoke with her earlier, but why was Jordan here as well?

"Ginny, Jordan's got some good news for you," Graham said.

Ginny looked to Jordan who looked like his normal serious self. "I just got word today that Carl pleaded guilty to several of the crimes we arrested him for. He's going away for a long time, Ginny. You're finally free."

Ginny blinked, unable to process everything Jordan had said. Carl was going to jail? She was free?

Graham crossed to her and placed his hands on her arms. "Ginny, are you okay? That's supposed to be good news."

"It's great news. I just can't believe it. Thank you. Thank you both."

Jordan nodded. "You're welcome. Now, I do believe my brother has another surprise for you, so I'm going to take his place managing the restaurant and leave you two alone."

Ginny watched him leave and then turned back to Graham. "Another surprise? What could be better than the news you just gave me?"

Graham's eyes twinkled, but he just shrugged. "Guess you'll have to follow me and see." He removed his hands from her arms, taking her hand with one of his.

Curious, Ginny let him lead her out of the restaurant and toward the small gazebo that sat in the park near the restaurant. A small table sat in the center of the gazebo, draped in a white lace tablecloth with two wrapped boxes on top.

"What is this, Graham?"

"Well, a little birdie told me it was your birthday. I wasn't sure if you would want a big party though I can throw one if you'd like, but I wanted to give you a few gifts just in case."

Tears pricked Ginny's eyes at his thoughtfulness. "I'm so surprised you even asked. I haven't had a birthday party in years, so thank you for not throwing something big. That might have been too much for me, but maybe we can do something small in the next few days. You and Tia and Cara and Jordan. Maybe a few others."

"That sounds like a plan." He picked up a small, rectangular box from the table and held it out to her. "Open this one first. I'm hoping you'll get some use out of it this weekend." His lips mashed together, but Ginny did not miss the twitching at the corners.

Gingerly, she peeled the paper back and opened the box. The words Holy Bible stared up at her in gold lettering from the soft black of the leather cover. Her heart tightened at the weight of the words in her hands. Though it had taken some discussions with Graham, she had finally decided to let Jesus into her heart, and she had found the same peace he had. Her eyes traveled to the bottom corner where more gold lettering caught her eye. Ginny Darling. Her name. She couldn't remember the last time she had owned a book, much less one with her name on it.

"Thank you." Her throat constricted with emotion and one tiny tear trickled down her cheek but not from sadness.

"Hey, none of that." He reached out and wiped the tear from her cheek with the pad of his thumb.

"Don't worry," she said with a soft smile, "it's a happy tear."

His own lips pulled into a smile. "Good, because there's one more gift." He picked up the smaller box and held it out to her.

Ginny repeated the process with the smaller box and

opened it to find a small golden cross with a heart across the center. This time she couldn't stop the tears from spilling out of her eyes. Carl had never given her jewelry and certainly never anything so beautiful. "This is…."

"It's a cross so you always remember how much Jesus loves you." He took the necklace from her and fastened it around her neck.

Ginny shivered at the soft touch of his fingers. "And the heart?"

"That's so you'll remember how much I love you, Ginny Darling." His hand caressed her cheek, and his eyes peered directly into her soul.

Her breath caught in her throat, and before she could think about it, before she could talk herself out of it, the words, "I love you too," spilled from her lips.

Graham's smile deepened as his face came closer to hers. Her eyes closed just before his lips touched hers, sending tingles through her body and down to her toes. Ginny had often dreamed of a kiss like this - the kind that made goosebumps erupt on her flesh, the kind that seared its way into her mind - but this was better even than she could have imagined, and she knew that she would be forever changed by it.

The End!

10
AUTHOR'S NOTE

When I was first approached to write in the Love under Lockdown series, I wasn't sure I could do it. I am so tired of being locked down, of not being able to attend my gym, cut my hair, or go to church, but I finally decided I could write it if I could make it suspenseful.

The town of Fire Beach has become dear to me, and when I first introduced Graham in book one, Fire Games, I hoped he would have a story one day. I'm glad I got to put it in this set.

I hope you enjoyed this story. If you did, would you do me a favor? Please leave a review. It really helps. It doesn't have to be long - just a few words to help other readers know what they're getting.

I'd love to hear from you, not only about this story, but about the characters or stories you'd like read in the future. I'm always looking for new ideas and if I use one of your characters or stories, I'll send you a free ebook and paperback of the book with a special dedication. Write to me at loranahoopes@gmail.com. And if you'd like to see what's coming next, be sure to stop by authorloranahoopes.com

I also have a weekly newsletter that contains many wonderful things like pictures of my adorable children, chances to win awesome prizes, new releases and sales I might be holding, great books from other authors, and anything else that strikes my fancy and that I think you would enjoy. I'll even send you the first chapter of my newest (maybe not even released yet) book if you'd like to sign up.

Even better, I solemnly swear to only send out one newsletter a week (usually on Tuesday unless life gets in the way which with three kids it usually does). I will not spam you, sell your email address to solicitors or anyone else, or any of those other terrible things.

This series will be continued, but for now, would you like to meet some characters for a new series.

PRAYERS AND BLESSINGS,
    Lorana

11
NOT READY TO SAY GOODBYE YET?

LOVE ON THE RUN IS BOOK 3.5 IN THE MEN OF FIRE Beach series. I'm hard at work on book 4

Secrets and Suspense will be the next book in the series. If you read, Never Forget the Past, you'll see that Cara was found unconscious on the floor of her bed and breakfast…

Secrets and Suspense

SHE'S EX-MILITARY OR IS SHE?

Cara Hunter owns the local bed and breakfast in Fire Beach, but when she's found unconscious on the floor, questions begin to surface about her past

He's a criminal investigator

Cole Davenport showed up in Fire Beach to arrest Cara Hunter, but is she really the victim?

When the truth comes out….

When the world Cara knew begins falling apart, who will she be able to trust?

Read on for a taste of Secrets and Suspense….

12
SECRETS AND SUSPENSE PREVIEW

"Steve, are you in here?" Cara Hunter knocked softly on Sergeant Steve Steele's door. A feeling of unease washed over her as it creaked open. Steve never left his door unlocked. Like her, he was paranoid of being caught doing his research. Even though they'd been sanctioned by the military, what they were doing could be dangerous if it fell into the wrong hands. It was something she worried about everyday, and she'd had enough conversations with Steve to know the fear had taken residence in his mind too.

She should turn around right now. Or call Jordan. At least if she had a detective with her, she wouldn't be blamed for whatever she might find inside, but she had to know. Careful not to touch anything more, she pulled her sleeves down over her hands and nudged the door open a little farther with her elbow.

The unease burgeoned into terror as she took in the room. Or what was left of it. Furniture had been shredded and lay upended across the room. Drawers hung like broken arms from the desk. Books and papers littered the floor, and an eerie silence filled the room. How she wished she had more than the small knife concealed in her boot.

The desire to call Steve's name again burned in her throat, but she clamped her jaws shut. Though it felt as if whoever had done this was gone, alerting them to her presence felt reckless in case they were still in the house.

Instead, she took ginger steps around the mess, careful not to step on anything and leave bookmarks. The living room opened to a kitchen which was equally messy. All the drawers had been emptied on the floor and the cabinet doors gaped open like hungry mouths. Someone had obviously been looking for something, and Cara knew they had probably found it.

Steve did most of his research in a hidden closet in his bedroom, but if whoever had done this was this thorough, it was unlikely they hadn't found the room. She just hoped Steve hadn't been home when they had.

Exiting the kitchen, she walked carefully down the hallway. Steve's house was small - just a single bedroom after he and his wife had split up. That left only two more doors - the bathroom and the bedroom. Both doors were open, and Cara glanced quickly in the sparse bathroom before continuing to the bedroom.

Fear, rage, and disgust battled for her dominant emotion as she nudged the bedroom door open further and saw Steve lying facedown on the bed. The puddle of brick colored liquid surrounding him left no doubt that he was dead, and the open door to his secret closet at the other end of the room confirmed her suspicion that his research was gone.

There was no reason to stay any longer. She needed to get out of here before anyone saw her and tried to pin this murder on her.

Retracing her steps, Cara exited the house and climbed back in her car. The composure she had worked so hard to contain while in the house crumbled as her door shut. Someone had killed Steve. Was she next?

Her hand shook as she fumbled to get the key in the ignition. She needed to call Jordan and have him send someone to the scene, but first she needed to call Malone. She had to know if he knew and what he was going to do to protect the rest of them.

She punched in his personal number before throwing the car into reverse and backing away from the crime scene. Every nerve in her body wanted her to flee, press the gas and roar out of the area, but that would only draw unwanted attention. Attention she didn't need.

"Cara? What's going on?" The concern in Malone's

deep voice resonated through her car, but it did nothing to calm her racing heart.

"Steve's dead." Choked with emotion, the strangled words hardly sounded like her voice.

"What?"

"He's dead. I stopped in for our monthly meetup, but I was too late. Someone beat me there. They trashed the place, killed Steve, and stole the research." Her hands gripped the steering wheel, the color in her knuckles fading to a dull white.

"Are you sure they got the research?"

Cara glanced down at her phone briefly as if glaring at it could send her ire to Malone. How could he sound so calm when she had just told him a member of their team was dead? And why did he appear more interested in the research than the man's life?

"Well, I didn't paw through everything and leave my fingerprints all over the place, but the house was trashed. His secret room was open. I have no doubt they found everything they were looking for. Do you even care about Steve?"

Malone's sigh echoed through her speakers. "Of course I do, but I don't have to remind you Cara that our work is important. We're talking about saving lives."

"Right now we ought to be thinking about endangering lives. Steve had samples of the virus which means someone else now has them, and we have no idea what they plan to do with them. What if they come after the rest of us? What if they come after me? Geez, Malone, how did they even know to come after Steve?" The questions tumbled out of her mouth like drips from a leaky faucet, but for each one she voiced, a dozen more scrambled for space in her brain.

"I don't know, Cara. I will look into it. For now, stay safe and see if you can get me that vaccine."

She wanted to ask him how exactly she was supposed to do that, but before she could say anything more, the click of him hanging up the phone reverberated through the car. She was on her own.

Well, not entirely on her own. She had Jordan and the rest of her friends in Fire Beach. They didn't know about her secret life, but she had no doubt they would help her out when she told them. She just had to make it back home.

Click here to continue reading Secrets and Suspense.

13
A FREE STORY FOR YOU

Enjoyed this story? Not ready to quit reading yet? If you sign up for my newsletter, you will receive The Billionaire's Impromptu Bet right away as my thank you gift for choosing to hang out with me.

The Billionaire's Impromptu Bet

A SWAT officer. A bored billionaire heiress. A bet that could change everything….

Read on for a taste of The Billionaire's Impromptu Bet….

14

THE BILLIONAIRE'S IMPROMPTU BET PREVIEW

Brie Carter fell back spread eagle on her queen-sized canopy bed sending her blond hair fanning out behind her. With a large sigh, she uttered, "I'm bored."

"How can you be bored? You have like millions of dollars." Her friend, Ariel, plopped down in a seated position on the bed beside her and flicked her raven hair off her shoulder. "You want to go shopping? I hear Tiffany's is having a special right now."

Brie rolled her eyes. Shopping? Where was the excitement in that? With her three platinum cards, she could go shopping whenever she wanted. "No, I'm bored with shopping too. I have everything. I want to do something exciting. Something we don't normally do."

Brie enjoyed being rich. She loved the unlimited credit

cards at her disposal, the constant apparel of new clothes, and of course the penthouse apartment her father paid for, but lately, she longed for something more fulfilling.

Ariel's hazel eyes widened. "I know. There's a new bar down on Franklin Street. Why don't we go play a little game?"

Brie sat up, intrigued at the secrecy and the twinkle in Ariel's eyes. "What kind of game?"

"A betting game. You let me pick out any man in the place. Then you try to get him to propose to you."

Brie wrinkled her nose. "But I don't want to get married." She loved her freedom and didn't want to share her penthouse with anyone, especially some man.

"You don't marry him, silly. You just get him to propose."

Brie bit her lip as she thought. It had been awhile since her last relationship and having a man dote on her for a month might be interesting, but.... "I don't know. It doesn't seem very nice."

"How about I sweeten the pot? If you win, I'll set you up on a date with my brother."

Brie cocked her head. Was she serious? The only thing Brie couldn't seem to buy in the world was the affection of Ariel's very handsome, very wealthy, brother. He was a movie star, just the kind of person Brie could consider marrying in the future. She'd had a crush on him as long as she and Ariel had been friends, but he'd always seen her as just that, his little sister's friend. "I thought you didn't want me dating your brother."

"I don't." Ariel shrugged. "But he's between girlfriends right now, and I know you've wanted it for ages. If you win this bet, I'll set you up. I can't guarantee any more than one date though. The rest will be up to you."

Brie wasn't worried about that. Charm she possessed in abundance. She simply needed some alone time with him, and she was certain she'd be able to convince him they were meant to be together. "All right. You've got a deal."

Ariel smiled. "Perfect. Let's get you changed then and see who the lucky man will be.

A tiny tug pulled on Brie's heart that this still wasn't right, but she dismissed it. This was simply a means to an end, and he'd never have to know.

JESSE CALHOUN RELAXED AS THE RHYTHMIC THUDDING OF the speed bag reached his ears. Though he loved his job, it was stressful being the SWAT sniper. He hated having to take human lives and today had been especially rough. The team had been called out to a drug bust, and Jesse was forced to return fire at three hostiles. He didn't care that they fired at his team and himself first. Taking a life was always hard, and every one of them haunted his dreams.

"You gonna bust that one too?" His co-worker Brendan

appeared by his side. Brendan was the opposite of Jesse in nearly every way. Where Jesse's hair was a dark copper, Brendan's was nearly black. Jesse sported paler skin and a dusting of freckles across his nose, but Brendan's skin was naturally dark and freckle free.

Jesse flashed a crooked grin, but kept his eyes on the small, swinging black bag. The speed bag was his way to release, but a few times he had started hitting while still too keyed up and he had ruptured the bag. Okay, five times, but who was counting really? Besides, it was a better way to calm his nerves than other things he could choose. Drinking, fights, gambling, women.

"Nah, I think this one will last a little longer." His shoulders began to burn, and he gave the bag another few punches for good measure before dropping his arms and letting it swing to a stop. "See? It lives to be hit at least another day." Every once in a while, Jesse missed training the way he used to. Before he joined the force, he had been an amateur boxer, on his way to being a pro, but a shoulder injury had delayed his training and forced him to consider something else. It had eventually healed, but by then he had lost his edge.

"Hey, why don't you come drink with us?" Brendan clapped a hand on Jesse's shoulder as they headed into the locker room.

"You know I don't drink." Jesse often felt like the outsider of the team. While half of the six-man team was married, the other half found solace in empty bottles and meaningless relationships. Jesse understood that - their job was such that they never knew if they would come home night after night - but he still couldn't partake.

Brendan opened his locker and pulled out a clean shirt. He peeled off his current one and added deodorant before tugging on the new one. "You don't have to drink. Look, I won't drink either. Just come and hang out with us. You have no one waiting for you at home."

That wasn't entirely true. Jesse had Bugsy, his Boston Terrier, but he understood Brendan's point. Most days, Jesse went home, fed Bugsy, made dinner, and fell asleep watching TV on the couch. It wasn't much of a life. "All right, I'll go, but I'm not drinking."

Brendan's lips pulled back to reveal his perfectly white teeth. He bragged about them, but Jesse knew they were veneers. "That's the spirit. Hurry up and change. We don't want to leave the rest of the team waiting."

"Is everyone coming?" Jesse pulled out his shower necessities. Brendan might feel comfortable going out with just a new application of deodorant, but Jesse needed to wash more than just dirt and sweat off. He needed to wash the sound of the bullets and the sight of lifeless bodies from his mind.

"Yeah, Pat's wife is pregnant again and demanding some crazy food concoctions. Pat agreed to pick them up if she let him have an hour. Cam and Jared's wives are having a girls' night, so the whole gang can be together. It will be nice to hang out when we aren't worried about being shot at."

"Fine. Give me ten minutes. Unlike you, I like to clean up before I go out."

Brendan smirked. "I've never had any complaints. Besides, do you know how long it takes me to get my hair like this?"

Jesse shook his head as he walked into the shower, but he knew it was true. Brendan had rugged good looks and muscles to match. He rarely had a hard time finding a woman. Jesse on the other hand hadn't dated anyone in the last few months. It wasn't that he hadn't been looking, but he was quieter than his teammates. And he wasn't looking for right now. He was looking for forever. He just hadn't found it yet.

Click here to continue reading The Billionaire's Impromptu Bet.

THE STORY DOESN'T END!

You've met a few people and fallen in love….

I bet you're wondering how you can meet everyone else.

Star Lake Series:

Sealed with a Kiss: Meet the quirky cast of Star Lake and find out if Max and Layla will ever find love.

When Love Returns: Return to Star Lake to hear Presley's story and find out if she gets the second chance with her first love.

Once Upon a Star: Continue the journey when aspiring actress Audrey returns home with a baby. Will Blake finally get the nerve to share his feelings with her?

Love Conquers All: Meet Lanie Perkins Hall who never imagined being divorced at thirty or falling for an old friend, but will his secrets keep them apart?

The Star Lake Collection: Get the latter three stories in one place. Series will include book 1 when it releases around November 2020.

The Heartbeats Series:

Where It All Began: Sandra Baker finds forgiveness and healing even after making a horrible choice.

The Power of Prayer: Will Callie Green find true love or be defined by her mistake?

When Hearts Collide: When Amanda Adams goes to college, she finds a world she was not ready for. But will she also find true love?

A Past Forgiven: Jess Peterson has lived a life of abuse and lost her self worth, but when she finds herself pregnant, will she find new hope?

The Heartbeats Collection: Grab all four Heartbeats novels in one collection

Sweet Billionaires Series:

The Billionaire's Impromptu Bet: Can a spoiled rich girl change when a bet turns to love?

The Billionaire's Secret: Can a playboy settle down when he finds out he has a daughter who needs him?

A Brush with a Billionaire: What happens when a stuck up actor lands in a small town and needs help from a female mechanic?

The Billionaire's Christmas Miracle: A twist on a Cinderella story when a billionaire meets a woman who doesn't belong at the ball.

The Billionaire's Cowboy Groom: Will one night six years ago keep Carrie from finding true love?

The Cowboy Billionaire: Coming Soon!

The Billionaire's Bliss: This collection contains The Billionaire's Secret, The Billionaire's Christmas Miracle, and The Billionaire's Cowboy Groom

The Lawkeeper Series:

Lawfully Matched: When the man she agreed to marry turns out to have a dark past, will Kate have to return home or will she find love with her rescuer in this historical fiction?

Lawfully Justified: Can a bounty hunter and a widow find love together in this historical fiction?

The Scarlet Wedding: William and Emma are planning their wedding, but an outbreak and a return from his past force them to change their plans. Is a happily ever after still in their future in this historical fiction?

Lawfully Redeemed: What happens when a K9 cop falls for the brother of her suspect? Contemporary romance.

The Lawkeeper Collection: Get all four books in one collection

The Are You Listening Series:

The Still Small Voice: Will Jordan listen to God's prompting in this speculative fiction?

A Spark in the Darkness Will Jordan be able to help Raven before the rapture occurs?

Blushing Brides Series:

The Cowboy's Reality Bride: He's agreed to be the bachelor on a reality dating show, but what happens when he falls for a woman who's not one of the contestants?

The Reality Bride's Baby: Laney wants nothing more than a baby, but when she starts feeling dizzy is it pregnancy or something more serious?

The Producer's Unlikely Bride: What happens when a producer and an author agree to a fake relationship?

Ava's Blessing in Disguise: Five years after marriage, Ava faces a mysterious illness that threatens to ruin her career. Will she find out what it is?

The Soldier's Steadfast Bride: coming soon

The Men of Fire Beach

Fire Games: Cassidy returns home from Who Wants to Marry a Cowboy to find obsessive letters from a fan. The cop assigned to help her wants to get back to his case, but what she sees at a fire may just be the key he's looking for.

Lost Memories and New Beginnings: A doctor, a patient with no memory, the men out to get her. Can he keep her safe when he doesn't know who he's looking for?

When Questions Abound: A Companion story to Lost Memories. Told from Detective Graves' point of view.

Never Forget the Past: Fireman Bubba must confront his past in order to clear his name and save lives.

Love on the Run: Graham is forced into lockdown

with one of his employees. Will he be able to save her from her ex and will she steal his heart?

Secrets and Suspense: Cara Hunter is hiding something about her military past. When she's suspected of murder, will she be able to convince Cole she's the victim?

The Men of Fire Beach Collection: Books 1-3

Texas Tornadoes

Defending My Heart: Forced to confront his past, Emmitt finds news that will change his life.

Run With My Heart: Sentenced to community service, Tucker finds himself falling for the manager.

Love on the Line: Blaine has hired Kenzi to redo his cabin, but what happens when she finds his darkest secret?

Touchdown on Love: When Mason's injury throws him together with ex-girlfriend, will sparks fly again?

Second Chance Reception: Jefferson is hiding something. When he falls for the team cook, will he let her in?

Small Town Short Stories

Small Town Dreams

Small Town Second Chances

Small Town Rivals

Small Town Life

Life in a Small Town: All four stories in one collection

Stand Alones:

Love Renewed: This books is part of the multi author second chance series. When fate reunites high school sweethearts separated by life's choices, can they find a second chance at love at a snowy lodge amid a little mystery?

Her children's early reader chapter book series:
    The Wishing Stone #1: Dangerous Dinosaur
    The Wishing Stone #2: Dragon Dilemma
    The Wishing Stone #3: Mesmerizing Mermaids
    The Wishing Stone #4: Pyramid Puzzle
    The Wishing Stone Inspirations 1: Mary's Miracle
    To see a list of all her books

          authorloranahoopes.com
          loranahoopes@gmail.com

DISCUSSION QUESTIONS

1. What was your favorite scene in the book? What made it your favorite?

2. Did you have a favorite line in the book? What do you think made it so memorable?

3. Who was your favorite character in the book and why?

4. What do you think would be the hardest part about escaping abuse?

5. What did you learn about God from reading this book?

6. How can you use that knowledge in your life from now on?

7. What do you think would make the story even better?

ABOUT THE AUTHOR

Lorana Hoopes is an inspirational author originally from Texas but now living in the PNW with her husband and three children. When not writing, she can be seen kick-boxing at the gym, singing, or acting on stage. One day, she hopes to retire from teaching and write full time.

Printed in the USA
CPSIA information can be obtained
at www.ICGtesting.com
LVHW011942160724
785670LV00011B/464